To my dancing idols and inspirations

A Random House Australia book
Published by Random House Australia Pty Ltd
Level 3, 100 Pacific Highway, North Sydney NSW 2060
www.randomhouse.com.au

Penguin
Random House
RANDOM HOUSE BOOKS

First published by Random House Australia in 2015

Random House Books is part of the Penguin Random House group of companies whose addresses can be found at global.penguinrandomhouse.com

National Library of Australia
Cataloguing-in-Publication Entry

Author: Bound, Samantha-Ellen
Title: Dance till you drop
ISBN: 978 0 857983 725 (pbk)
Series: Silver shoes; 4
Target Audience: For primary-school age
Subjects: Dance – Juvenile fiction
         Dance – Competitions – Juvenile fiction
Dewey Number: A823.4

Cover and internal illustrations by J.Yi
Cover design by Kirby Armstrong
Internal design by Midland Typesetters, Australia
Printed in Australia by Griffin Press, an accredited ISO AS/NZS 14001:2004
Environmental Management System printer

Random House Australia uses papers that are natural, renewable and recyclable products and made from wood grown in sustainable forests. The logging and manufacturing processes are expected to conform to the environmental regulations of the country of origin.

Dance Till You Drop

SAMANTHA-ELLEN BOUND

RANDOM HOUSE AUSTRALIA

Chapter One

'You can't *what?*' Ellie crossed her arms and narrowed her big green eyes at me.

Uh-oh. I knew I was in trouble.

I looked at Ellie's fluoro-pink jazz boots. Then at Ashley's bag with the ripped handle. Then at the picture of a young Miss Caroline dancing on a cruise ship above the bluest water I'd ever seen.

But I couldn't look at Ellie.

'I can't come to your birthday party,' I whispered. 'I'm sorry.'

'Why not?' said Ellie.

I picked at my leotard. Then I gave a little cough. Wow. Sometimes Ellie can be scary when she's excited or passionate about something and can't stop talking. But when she's silent? That's terrifying.

'Well, come on, Paige,' said Ellie. 'You're supposed to be my best friend, and now you can't come to my eleventh birthday party? There better be a good reason.'

'Mum told me yesterday I have a ballroom competition,' I said. 'I'm really sorry, Ellie. You know how much I wanted to come.'

Eleanor is my best friend, so it wasn't a lie. We've been friends since we first began as tinies at our dance school, Silver Shoes.

Ellie is loud and energetic and never afraid. And that's why I love her – because she makes me feel less quiet and shy.

But you don't want to get in her bad books. And I think I just did.

'You already missed my singing showcase because you were doing some ballet workshop, and now you're going to miss my party because you've got a competition?'

'I can't help it,' I said.

'Paige,' huffed Ellie, shoving her foot into her jazz boot. 'I love dancing too, everyone knows that, but I don't let it get in the way of doing stuff with my friends.'

'I want to come!' I said. 'And I wanted to be at your singing showcase as well! But I'll get into trouble if I miss these ballroom things.'

'You can't miss this *one* ballroom competition?' asked Ellie. 'Even though you do, like, a thousand?'

'No,' I said.

'Why not?'

'It's really good practice. And exposure,' I explained, before realising I was just repeating what Mum always said.

I thought about my ballroom partner, Benji, and my cheeks grew warm.

'Also I can't let Benji down.'

'What about letting me down?' pouted Ellie, pulling on her other jazz boot.

I couldn't think of anything to say.

'Whatever,' she said, making a big deal of tying her final lace. She gave me a mean look as she breezed by me on her way out the door. 'You don't even like ballroom.'

That wasn't true! Was it?

I sure didn't like it when it caused fights with my best friend.

But Benji and I had been working so hard on our waltz for the ballroom competition. My mum was state waltz champion before I was born. I know it meant a lot to her that

Benji and I take out our age group at the competition. She made us practise in every spare moment – sometimes I felt I was even waltzing in my sleep!

I sighed and put Ellie's street clothes in a neat pile next to mine. Then I headed to the studio, ready for our weekly technique class. My arms were really sore from holding a ballroom stance for three hours. I hoped we didn't spend too much time on cartwheels and walkovers today.

'Paige!'

I looked into the open doorway and saw Mum waving at me from a sea of dresses. She's in charge of costumes at Silver Shoes.

'Your hair is a mess!' Mum scolded. 'Come here.'

'I'm late for class,' I began to say, but she'd already taken my hair – which is long, blonde and silky and ALWAYS falls out even if it's tied up – and twisted it into a bun so tight I felt like I had sunburn.

'Work on your walkovers today, honey,' Mum said, giving me a kiss. 'Your knees are always crooked.'

'Okay,' I said, and escaped before she could find an imaginary thread hanging loose on my leotard.

Once I was in the studio I went to take my usual place next to Ellie.

But she wasn't there. She was over in the far corner, laughing with our friend, Ash.

I guessed she was still mad, then.

Luckily our other friend, Riley, came rushing in, trying to fix her curly hair into a braid.

'Hey Paige,' she said, stopping next to me. 'Whoops. Late again.' She gave me a big smile that said she didn't really care if she was late or not.

I decided to copy her and spend the class not caring.

But I did care.

I cared that my knees stayed crooked on the walkovers. I cared that I got so dizzy in my pirouettes I almost crashed into the mirror.

And I cared that throughout the whole class, Ellie didn't look at me once.

Chapter Two

The next day, Friday, I had ballroom practice after school.

I walked into the back studio to find Benji standing stiffly in front of the mirror, his chin up and arms out.

Benji doesn't take any other classes at Silver Shoes. He's in a hip hop group with Ash, but that's outside of the studio.

I hung back in the doorway, embarrassed – for myself or for him, I didn't know.

When he caught me looking though, his body collapsed like jelly that's just been punched.

'Hey,' he said.

'Hi,' I said, coming into the studio. 'What were you doing?'

'Working on my posture,' Benji said. 'Mum said it's no good. Said there's too much hip hop slouch.'

'Oh,' I said.

'What about you?' he asked. 'Do you think when I dance ballroom I'm too hip hoppy?'

'Oh,' I squeaked. 'No. I don't think so.'

I really wasn't sure, because when I danced with Benji my head got all messed up and I couldn't really think about anything except trying not to step on his feet.

He shrugged. 'I don't care. Not gonna be a ballroom dancer, anyway.'

'Well, don't tell your mum that,' I said, sitting down on the floor to stretch out my feet. 'Don't tell mine, either. In her mind, we're together for life.' I flushed bright red. 'As dance partners, I mean!'

Benji collapsed on the floor and lounged about next to me. I moved my legs away so that my feet weren't touching him. He kept staring at himself in the mirror.

'We've got that ballroom comp coming up,' I said, because the silence was making my fingers and toes itch.

Benji nodded. 'Yeah.'

'I'm missing Ellie's birthday because of it.'

Benji sat straighter and squared his shoulders, but he didn't look away from his reflection. 'Yeah?'

'She's pretty mad.'

'Yeah?'

'I hope it doesn't turn into a big fight,' I said, pulling up my tights.

Gosh! Why was it so hard to talk to boys!

Benji was pulling ridiculous stage faces in the mirror now. 'Yeah?' he said, again. 'Don't do the ballroom comp then. I don't mind. We do a hundred others.'

'I can't just pull out,' I said.

'Why?' asked Benji, swishing his hair back in an over-the-top way.

'Because I have to do the comp,' I said.

'Have to or *want* to?' asked Benji.

I looked down at my toes. 'Want to,' I said.

But the ticklish feeling in my tummy said I wasn't so sure. If I didn't feel excited about it, why was I doing it?

'Are you sure?' said Benji, flicking his eyes at me in the mirror.

Gosh! Maybe Benji hated dancing with me because I was so terrible and *he* wanted to pull out!

But I didn't get to ask him because Mum and our ballroom teacher, Fleur, came in.

'What's this?' Mum laughed. 'On the floor will never do. We better get you up and dancing, hey?'

Benji gave her a weird smile that his eyes didn't agree with.

'How are you, Benji?' asked Mum. She kissed him on the top of his head, and the way he tried to duck out of it made me smile. 'You ready to dance the waltz with my Paigey?'

'I guess,' he said.

'I guess!' Mum laughed again. 'Well, I hope you guessed right, because we're going to make you two state champions!'

'Great,' I heard Benji mumble under his breath.

Fleur is a nice teacher, but Mum usually ends up taking over. She calls out corrections from the chair at the side of the studio, or jumps up to partner Fleur to show us how it's done.

Most of the time I wish Mum would go away to fix up the costumes or something, because I don't feel like I dance my best when she's around.

I think she forgets that Benji and I are only just learning ballroom. We haven't been doing it for twenty years, like she did. And she keeps slamming us with new styles to learn when we really should be concentrating on just a few.

Take this example. Fleur was getting Benji and me to do some slow circles around the studio, in a basic one, two, three; one, two, three box step. It was just a warm-up! But Mum called out, 'Paigey, you've got to stand closer to Benji! He's not contagious, sweetheart, you can't be ten metres away from him – it ruins the line of your arms.'

I know it's meant to be encouraging, but I get nervous when she calls out stuff like that!

And when I did move closer to Benji I got all stiff because I felt like it still wasn't good enough.

Plus I didn't like being too near to Benji. I wasn't sure which part of his face I was meant to look at. We were so close I could see a chip on his front left tooth. Imagine what he could see on mine! I hope I didn't have a booger!

Benji acts cool, but he's really good at ballroom. His thing is hip hop, but his mum and mine know each other from the old dancing days, so they thought it would be a great idea to get us together as ballroom partners.

Benji's a natural. Sometimes he looks like he enjoys himself, even with me stumbling and turning the wrong way and treading on his toes.

I couldn't understand why I was so bad. I bet Riley or Ellie wouldn't have the same problem. Mum would never yell things out at them!

Great. So I'd miss Ellie's birthday to do a ballroom competition that I wasn't even good at. It just got worse and worse.

Chapter Three

'I'm so glad we made it in time! How are you going, sweetie? Closing soon?' Mum asked the girl behind the counter.

We were at the Danceworks store, and the girl (it was Ash's big sister, Bridget) looked up from where she was tagging singlets.

'Half an hour,' Bridget said. 'Hey Paige.'

'Hello,' I said.

'You guys know what you're after?'

'Absolutely,' said Mum. 'Hairnets. Paige's hair just won't stay still! And a nice, plain leotard with a sweetheart neckline.' Mum turned to me. 'Paigey, that's what I'm going to create your waltz costume around. Do we need anything else, bub? You excited?'

'I guess so,' I said, but Mum was already flicking through the racks.

I already had about five unused leotards at home, so I didn't see why I couldn't use one of them.

'We're going for a music-box theme, Paigey,' said Mum, holding up a long-sleeved number and then putting it back. 'Benji's mum and I were talking. He'll be the soldier and you'll be the music-box ballerina. We reckon a lovely, soft yellow for the base colour? Some emerald greens in the skirt – that'll make your eyes pop. What do you think, honey?'

'Yellow's nice,' I said, yawning.

There were two fluoro-pink glittery dance tanks hanging next to me that I knew Ellie would love.

Even though she hadn't talked to me since technique class on Thursday.

'Then we'll do some gold detailing,' babbled Mum, 'and use creamy white chiffon for the layers in your skirt, set against the green. I was at the craft store today and I saw some stunning silk butterflies for your hair. The wings were trimmed with these tiny crystals, so when you moved them it looked like they were flying and leaving a sparkly trail. You'll be such a vision, babe!'

Mum looked at me. I realised I'd been staring at the tanks, thinking about Ellie.

'What's wrong, honey?' said Mum.

'I'm just really tired,' I said.

'Of course you are, darling,' said Mum, kneeling down to me with a leotard clutched in her fist. 'You've been dancing all week, and you've had those extra ballroom practices, too. I'm so proud of your dedication.'

'I haven't been doing that well in ballet,' I confessed. 'I think Ms McGlone is mad at me.'

'Rubbish,' said Mum. 'You should be mad at her for not making you the Ice Queen in the eisteddfod. You would have been better than Jasmine. Lovely girl, but . . .'

Jasmine is ten times better than me at ballet (and she knows it). She deserved the lead. And it doesn't bother me if I don't get the starring roles. It's a lot of pressure. I get so nervous as it is!

But Mum thinks I'm being under-used. Also, she doesn't like Mrs de Lacy, Jasmine's mum. She said Mrs de Lacy is a pushy know-it-all, and that she thinks Silver Shoes was created just to promote the talents of Jasmine.

'A true stage mum, Paigey,' she told me once. 'But I don't want to talk about it. Negative thoughts give you wrinkles.'

'Anyway,' said Mum, looking at the leotard she was holding, 'the colour of this one's nice, but I don't like the cut. Might have to try Transitions Dancewear.'

'Do I have to do the ballroom competition?' I blurted out.

Mum paused. There was silence in the shop. Bridget disappeared out the back.

'Why did you say that?' asked Mum. 'Of course you have to do the competition! You've been so excited. And you can't let down Benji.'

'He doesn't care,' I said.

'Yes he does, Paige. Don't be silly.' She started looking through the costumes again very loudly. A coathanger fell on the ground.

'It's just that Ellie's birthday party is on the same day,' I said.

'Ellie will have plenty of other birthday parties,' said Mum.

'But I really want to go,' I said, unable to stop myself talking. 'I'm already dancing every single day, but I still don't think I'm good enough for the comp. Not yet, anyway.'

'Yes you are,' Mum said. 'You're my daughter, aren't you?'

'But Ellie's birthday . . .' I said.

'That's enough, Paige,' said Mum, firmly. 'You're just tired. We'll get you a hairnet and then we'll go home and I'll make you a nice quinoa salad for tea.'

'But . . .'

'You don't have time to think about birthday parties anyway,' Mum continued. 'You need to focus. The Royal Academy of Ballet is holding a masterclass weekend in June and it's very respected. I've already signed you up for an audition next Sunday.'

As if this week wasn't bad and busy enough, now I had to worry about a masterclass?

Worst of all, Mum had just dropped one of my most hated words:

Audition.

Chapter Four

'Hello, my name's Paige Montreal, I'm ten years old, and my favourite style of dance is lyrical.'

I thought about it a bit more.

'Actually, it's ballet.'

If I was going to audition for a ballet masterclass, I'd better say my favourite style was ballet!

I looked at myself in the mirror of the drama studio at Silver Shoes – a small blonde scaredy-cat. And I was only practising for the audition. It wasn't even the real thing.

I stood up straighter. I tried to hold my head in the confident way that Riley did. I pretended to hold a barre, bent my legs into plié position, and raised my arms into port de bras.

But I had big dark circles under my eyes. And my shoulders had a tired slope to them. My legs wouldn't maintain turn-out either.

Riley poked her head around the door. 'Paige?'

I jumped. 'Oh, hi,' I said. 'What are you doing?'

'Looking for you,' said Riley. 'Class is about to start. What are you doing?'

'Trying to be like you,' I said.

'What?' she asked, taking a step inside.

'Nothing,' I said.

'You okay?'

Riley came and stood next to me. Her hair was messy, like she'd been running around outside for two hours. Mine was back in its usual too-tight bun, tied with a new pink ribbon.

She tried to smooth her hair down and then gave up. 'Who cares,' she said, when she saw me looking. 'I dance with my feet, not my hair.'

Our ballet teacher, Ms McGlone, likes us to look very prim and proper in class. That means exactly the right colour leotard, no ripped tights, clean slippers and tidy hair. I'm too scared to look anything but perfect. Ms McGlone is tough!

But Riley doesn't always follow the rules. A few weeks ago she forgot her tights and Ms McGlone said she couldn't take class.

Riley just shrugged and walked out as if she didn't care. I would have died!

'I saw Ellie out there,' said Riley. 'She's here for some musical theatre thing.'

'Oh,' was all I could say.

Ellie had ignored me at school. We usually do everything together. But at lunchtime, when we were with our group of friends, the only time she looked at me was to roll her eyes when I said I didn't feel like playing chasings with the boys.

What I really wanted to do was go to the library and take a nap. It was only Monday, but I already felt like it was the end of the week.

'You really okay?' Riley asked again. 'You look kind of . . . dead.'

'I'm a bit tired,' I said. 'Yesterday Mum made me practise an audition piece for that ballet masterclass at Dance Art. Are you going?'

Dance Art Academy is Silver Shoes' rival dance school. It's a big, rich school with about a million students – they often win at competitions and eisteddfods.

Mum says that even with their fancy reputation she would never send me there because I wouldn't get the quality attention I get at Silver Shoes. Also, she and Miss Caroline are friends from way back when they both used to dance professionally.

I don't want to go to Dance Art anyway. Those girls are scary. It's like a tribe of mini Jasmines.

'Yeah, I saw that,' Riley said. 'Ms McGlone put my name down. She stopped me and Jasmine after class.'

'It sounds very posh,' I said.

'Yeah, I guess,' Riley said. 'It would be cool to do it but I'm not fussed.' She shrugged. 'Come on, you got any snakes? I need the sugar.'

Lolly snakes are our thing – mine, and Riley, Ellie and Ash's. We always have a packet on the go. It was my turn to bring them and I'd come prepared. We went to the change room and I rummaged through my dance bag (it has Cabbage Patch Kids on it – I've collected the dolls since I was little!) until I found the packet. Riley picked green. I picked red.

Ellie came in while we were munching on the snakes. She was singing to herself. Her voice was getting better. But she stopped when she saw us and her face went blank.

'Hi Riley,' she said.

Nothing for me.

Ellie came right over to where I was sitting but all she did was pick up a pair of chorus shoes that were on the bench. I saw she'd added tiny pink bows near the buckle. It was such an Ellie thing to do.

It made me really miss her.

'You want a snake?' I asked, holding out the packet.

'Gross,' said Ellie. She got the shoes and then glanced at my dance bag. 'Lame,' she said, although she'd never seemed to have a problem with it before. Then she spun on her heel and stalked off. 'See ya,' she said to Riley on her way out.

The snakes tipped over onto the bench and fell on the floor. My heart sank right along with them.

Chapter Five

On Tuesday morning my eyes felt like they'd been stuck together with fake eyelash glue. Even my backpack felt heavier as I trudged into school. It was only as I went to sit down at my desk that I noticed I had two different socks on.

Boy, was I tired. After ballet I'd stayed up late to finish off my school project because I didn't get a chance to do it on the weekend with all that dancing.

Plus I'd been having the worst dreams. Nightmares about dancing witches, but also awful ones where I was at the ballroom competition and bad things kept happening. My skirt was tucked up into my leotard, or the audience started throwing old pointe shoes at me, or I kept treading on Benji's feet so much that I broke all his toes.

Benji is also in my class at school, Our Lady of Lourdes. When I saw him at his desk I flushed bright red, as if he'd read my mind and found out I'd been dreaming about him.

At school we sit in a table of four, which changes every month. The current arrangement is two boys and two girls on each table. Ellie and I share a desk with these two boys, Larry and Rowan, who are best friends.

Somehow they'd realised Ellie and I were having a fight. All week they'd been saying stupid things and pretending to be overly polite to each other. Then they'd look at us and collapse into giggles.

Once upon a time, Ellie would have rolled her eyes at such silliness. Now she laughed right along with them. She wouldn't look at me, even though we sat opposite each other.

During maths, the most boring subject in the world, she still didn't make eye contact, and Larry and Rowan were cheating off each other on the maths problems. So I had nothing to do but look down at my desk.

All the ends of the numbers grew little hands and feet and started dancing across my page. There were tap shoes, ballet slippers, chorus shoes, hip hop sneakers, pointe shoes and more.

I wished I could dance away with them.

After maths and after either Larry or Rowan farted loudly and tried to blame it on the other, we had Australian history, where we were learning about famous national figures.

But I soon realised I wasn't listening to our teacher, Mr Herbert, at all. I wasn't doing anything.

There was a strange buzzing in my head. The other kids went out of focus until I could only see bits of them, like a nose or a finger, or the tip of an ear.

In the middle of it all, I thought, *Do I even want to dance?*

It was the scariest thought I'd ever had. Scarier than waiting to go on stage. Scarier than an audition.

My head drooped forward but I caught it in time and tried to focus on Mr Herbert. But then it nodded again and I felt my body slump forward. I was half-aware of falling into Rowan.

He turned around quickly and looked at me like I'd just appeared from another planet.

'I'm sorry,' I whispered. 'I didn't mean to.'

Larry grinned at him. 'She's falling for you, Row,' he whispered.

'No, it was an accident!' I said.

'Can you shut up?' Ellie hissed at us. 'I'm trying to listen.'

But she wasn't, really. I saw her notebook; it was covered in drawings of dance costumes.

I sat quietly then and tried to focus on Fred Hollows and Banjo Paterson and how they'd contributed to Australia. Ellie raised her hand.

'What about famous Australian dancers?' she said.

I waited for Mr Herbert's answer. But it was no good. First, one arm went across my desk. I lowered my head onto it. Then my eyes closed. And then . . .

'Paige!'

'Huh?'

'Paige, you're talking out loud! Wake up!'

Somebody shook me awake. It took me two seconds to work out where I was and what had happened.

Oh gosh. This was worse than an audition or forgetting the steps on stage. Falling asleep in class and then sleep-talking out loud. And everyone was looking!

I began to feel sick. Rowan and Larry were giggling. Benji was watching me. And when I dared to glance at Ellie, I found her staring at me, too.

She took her hand off my arm. I saw a speck of worry in her eyes and then she rolled them again, crossed her arms and faced the front.

'Paige?' said Mr Herbert. 'Are you all right? Do you need water and some fresh air?'

'Yes,' I managed to squeak.

'Can someone take Paige outside for five minutes?' Mr Herbert asked the class.

I looked at Ellie, but her eyes were glued to the whiteboard.

'I'll do it,' said Benji. He pushed back his chair. 'Come on, Paige.'

He grabbed a glass of water from the sink and I followed him outside. I wanted to cry and die of embarrassment all at once.

'You okay?' he asked me, as we sat down on a bench in the courtyard.

I just nodded and took the water.

I was so horrified at falling asleep and talking in class that I forgot to be uncomfortable about him sitting next to me and awkwardly patting my back.

I didn't think this was what Fleur had in mind when she told us that we had to work on being 'together'.

In fact, I was pretty sure Benji would never want to dance with me again.

Chapter Six

'No, no, Paige, you must centre your body! You cannot dip forward or back because that will unbalance Benji. You must move as one.'

I sighed. 'Sorry.'

Benji had been trying to spin me for fifteen minutes. It was only a one-legged standing spin, too – not even fancy – he basically stayed on the same spot, spinning me round and round.

But surprise, surprise, I couldn't do it. I kept tipping onto him. Or I'd get off balance and pull him forward as I tried to get back my centre of gravity.

'Try once more,' Fleur coaxed.

'I'm dizzy,' I said, 'and my back hurts. Benji's gripping too tight.'

Benji seemed surprised at that because he looked at me and then shifted his hands behind his back.

Great. Now he was upset at me, too. It wasn't even true. I just didn't want to keep spinning.

Fleur gave me a long look. 'All right,' she said. 'Let's have a short break. Then we'll try the spin again later. Okay?' She left the room, leaving me with Benji.

A huge silence fell around us, like that moment you watch someone forget the next step on stage.

'I didn't mean . . .' I started to say.

'I'm sorry,' he said at the same time.

'No, it was me,' I said.

'Are you okay from yesterday?' he asked.

Another silence.

'You weren't really hurting me then,' I said quickly, before he could get in. 'I just . . . I'm not very good, that spin . . . I'm a bit tired . . .'

'Yeah, sleeping in class.' He laughed. 'Pretty tired.'

'You didn't have to look after me,' I said. My shoes felt too tight and I suddenly had to loosen the buckle. 'But thank you.'

'Cool,' Benji said.

Cool? What was cool? That he didn't mind looking after me? Or that it was fine to fall asleep in class? Which one? Why are boys so hard to understand?

Fleur came back in then and clapped her hands to get our attention. Like we needed an excuse to not look at each other! Lucky we were all right dancing with each other because when it came to talking we didn't have a clue.

To give us a break from the lifts, Fleur made us practise our complete reverse turns (it basically means a fancy turn to change the direction you're going on the dance floor). She kept yelling: 'Paige, your head is facing the wrong way!' or 'Connect through the trunk, lean away at the chest' or 'That promenade must be closer!'

By that stage, Benji and I were dancing so close I could smell his shampoo. It smelled like apples and was nothing like what I imagined a boy would use.

'So have you two heard about the showcase?' Fleur asked before calling out, 'Wrong foot, Paige!'

Benji shrugged slightly, which caused me to tip forward again and I banged my forehead against his ear.

'Sorry!' I gasped.

I got no reply but swore I heard a little snicker.

Fleur meant the mid-year showcase coming up at Silver Shoes. Each class gave a preview of the current competition dance and some people could do duos or solos if they wanted to.

Ms McGlone had told us at ballet last night that they were recruiting for performers. I'd pushed it to the back of my mind. I didn't mind doing the group dances because I already knew them, but if Mum ever found out about it, she'd make me do something on my own. And I didn't want to. I didn't deserve to. Right now I couldn't bear the thought of any extra dance practice!

'Well, I was thinking it might be nice if you two did a ballroom routine,' said Fleur. 'A lot of people don't know you're taking private ballroom lessons. It'll be a nice surprise for the other kids.'

My heart sank a little, and so did my shoulders, because Fleur yelled out, 'Posture, Paige, watch your neck.'

I tried to flatten my back but only ended messing up the timing of my chassé.

Benji stopped dancing and stepped away from me. 'I'm not doing ballroom at the showcase,' he said.

Fleur threw up her hands. 'What do you mean?'

'I'm a hip hop dancer,' said Benji. 'I do hip hop. That's what I want to be known for. I'm doing *this* because Mum made me.'

Was Benji embarrassed that he was my ballroom partner? Did he hate dancing with me?

'What are you talking about?' asked Fleur. 'You enjoy the waltz, the tango, eh? The jive? I've taught you. You're a natural.'

'I don't care!' said Benji. 'No one listens. I don't want to do it!'

'Benji –'

'No!' shouted Benji.

Then he walked right out of the studio.

'He's just having a moment,' Fleur told me.

'May I go look for him?' I asked. 'I should see if he's okay.'

'Well, you can't waltz on your own,' said Fleur.

I stepped into the dark hallways of Silver Shoes. I felt bad. I was so worried and stressed out about my dancing that I hadn't really noticed Benji wasn't enjoying himself either.

I turned a corner and was just going past the costume room when I heard my name called out.

It was Mum.

Chapter Seven

'Paigey, come in here, I've got your costume all ready.'

'I can't, I'm looking for –'

'Come on, sweetie, you'll love it!'

Mum was surrounded by every colour you could imagine. There was tulle, silk, sequins, velvet, lycra and chiffon packed into every corner of the costume room. In her hands was my waltz dress.

So you know how our waltz had a music-box theme? I think Mum was inspired by that fairytale 'The Steadfast Tin Soldier', where the toy soldier falls in love with a paper ballerina. Except in our waltz, I was really upset at being stuck in the music box and Benji was the one who freed me.

For the costume, Mum had created an amazing fairy ballerina dress from that plain leotard she'd bought at Danceworks. She'd even added a tiny set of wings at the back. They were made out of scraps of chiffon and cotton wool, and decorated with tiny fake butterflies, rhinestones and dangling beads.

The leotard had green, gold and white sequinned beads over one shoulder, embroidered to look like wildflowers.

And the skirt! It was a big floating puff of yellow and white chiffon layers, some with a dash of the green sequinned beads.

It was *so* beautiful. I knew Mum had been working on it all weekend and yesterday. It was so nice of her. But it also meant another thing:

There was no way I could EVER pull out of the ballroom comp now.

'You're going to look so pretty with this dress. You'll win the comp for sure. How's it going with Fleur? Did you and Benji work on the spin?'

'Yes,' I said.

'Good,' Mum said. 'Come on, try it on. I want to see how it sits.'

'We're in the middle of practice,' I said.

'Oh really?' asked Mum. 'Because I just saw Benji run past the door so I thought you were taking a break.'

Uh-oh. There was something in Mum's voice that told me she had something up her sleeve.

Something that I wouldn't like.

I changed into the dress and straightaway had the 'costume effect'. That's where you immediately feel like you become the character you're dancing. I imagined my jewellery box with all the trinkets and love notes and old lipsticks around me.

Gosh it was a beautiful dress.

'So, Paigey . . .' said Mum, adjusting some beads on the shoulder-work.

She was so close I could see the creases in her eyelids where the eyeshadow was rubbing off.

'How come you didn't tell me that they're asking for dancers for the mid-year showcase?'

My mind blanked, like I really was a wind-up ballerina and the key had just run down.

'I forgot,' I said.

'You forgot?' said Mum.

'I think so,' I said. 'I've been so busy practising my audition for the masterclass that –'

'Don't you think it would be nice if you did something?' asked Mum. 'You want to get in quick, or the teachers will choose someone else. We can go tell Miss Caroline after class that you're interested.'

'But I'm not,' I said, surprising even myself.

'Pardon?' asked Mum. She stopped pinning and looked at me.

'Well, I'm already doing the group dances and I don't really have time to be practising anything else. Plus, there are other girls who are better than me who should have the chance to do a solo. I know Ellie wants to . . .'

'Nonsense!' said Mum. 'You're one of the best dancers at Silver Shoes. Of course you should have an extra dance.'

'I'm not really,' I said quietly.

'That's enough, Paige,' said Mum. 'You were born to dance. You're just like me when I was your age.'

'I'm not you, though,' I said.

Mum pretended not to hear that. Instead, she started tugging at the gold layers in my skirt. 'You and Benji should at least do some ballroom. Your Silver Shoes friends will want to see what you've been working on all year.'

'What about what I want?' I said, even more quietly, because it was getting hard to speak.

I don't know if that was because of how tight Mum had taken my dress in or if it was because of the bubble in my throat. I felt exhausted even thinking about more dancing.

'What did you just say?' said Mum, giving me another Mum look.

It looked like she was trying not to cry. I'm sure that was my imagination, but it did make me feel bad.

'Nothing.'

'Okay,' said Mum. 'Well, the dress looks stunning, babe; I'll just fix up these skirts a bit.'

'Thank you,' I said. Then we didn't say anything to each other while I got the costume off.

I left to go find Benji. But I had a yucky feeling, and all the magic of the dress had gone.

Chapter Eight

Benji was sitting outside on the old swing set, throwing bark at the bin.

'Rubbish only,' I said, pointing at the sign.

He laughed. 'Yeah, sorry for walking out,' he said. 'I just don't want to do ballroom in the showcase.'

'Are you embarrassed to dance with me?' I asked, sitting next to him. 'I know sometimes I'm not very good.'

'Nah, course not!' he said. 'Why do you always say that?'

'Well, when I compare myself to other girls, like Jasmine and Riley and Ellie, they're all so talented and they always win at competitions. I only ever get third, if anything.'

'That's because you take too many classes,' Benji said. 'If you focused on the styles you like the most, you'd probably get better at them.'

'Isn't it good to be an all-rounder?' I asked. I picked up some bark and began to throw it.

'Rubbish only,' said Benji, grinning.

'I'll throw you in there,' I said, grinning back.

Benji stuck out his chest. 'I do the lifts around here.'

'Oh no, dancing!' I exclaimed. 'That's what we're meant to be doing now.' I looked guiltily at the door, as if expecting Mum and Fleur to come charging out.

'It's more fun to throw bark at a bin,' grumbled Benji.

'Do you really hate ballroom that much?' I asked him.

He was quiet for a moment. 'I don't hate it. It's just . . .' he threw another piece of bark. It landed right inside the bin.

'Success!' he cried, throwing his arms up and almost falling off the swing. I giggled.

Benji settled himself back on the seat. 'Dunno, if it was my choice to do ballroom, I think I'd enjoy it more. But Mum made me do it because she thought I needed something to balance the hip hop. Like I'll turn into a gangster or something.'

'Why didn't you just say no?' I asked.

Benji snorted. 'Look who's talking.'

'I don't hate ballroom,' I protested, 'but I feel like I *have* to do it, which makes it less . . . fun.'

'That's exactly what I said, except more girly,' said Benji.

'Well, I am a girl,' I said.

What a stupid thing to say! I picked up a whole handful of bark and threw it at the bin to cover up my embarrassment. All the little bits bounced off the edge.

'Aw, come on,' said Benji. 'You're a bad shot!'

'So if you don't hate ballroom, are you embarrassed that people will find out you do it?' I asked.

'Nah, it's not that,' said Benji. 'I'm just sick of everything being ballroom, ballroom, ballroom. It's like, do this comp, learn tango, try the waltz, do the showcase. But no one actually asks me if I *want* to do it. No one seems to care that hip hop's my thing.' He shrugged. 'What about you?'

'I don't think I'm that good,' I said. 'Because I'm rushed off from class to class,

I don't get the time to focus on one thing. I'm stuffed full of tap and ballet and jazz and ballroom and masterclasses and showcases. All this dance stuff pushes out sleep, school, relaxing and . . . my best friend.'

I really missed Ellie. And here I was talking to Benji, like I would usually talk to her. Benji was cool, but he was a boy, and I didn't feel comfortable around him like I did with Ellie.

'Well, you know what we gotta do,' said Benji. 'We gotta stick together. We gotta say no to the showcase. We gotta be a team!'

He held out his hand to me in a mock superhero shake and it was dumb, because although I was practically glued to him when we were dancing, I felt really embarrassed to shake his hand.

I did, though. Very quickly.

'Hey,' he said, getting up off the swing. 'I got this hip hop gig at the community festival on Sunday. Wanna come? Ash is in it, too.'

'Oh,' I said, 'I can't. I have that ballet masterclass.'

'Your loss,' said Benji. 'Come on, we better go back or Fleur will lose it.'

Great. Something else I'm missing out on. And all because of a ballet masterclass I don't even want to do.

Was there such a thing as too much dance?

Chapter Nine

'The teacher said that my voice is twice as strong as it was two months ago, and that if I keep on with these vocal exercises, by the end of the year I could be going for lead roles instead of the chorus.'

Ellie's hands were going everywhere, the way they always do when she's excited. Her long hair was done up in two braids with pink ribbon woven through them. She also had pink and purple leg warmers on over her stockings.

'This leotard keeps giving me a wedgie,' said Ashley. 'Who brought the snakes? I'm starving.'

'Ash, you ate my sandwich five minutes ago,' said Riley.

'And that works out really well for me,' Ellie pushed on, 'because there's this musical coming up and I want to try out for it because it's going to tour schools . . .' She trailed into silence as she noticed me standing by the door. 'Oh, never mind.'

'Paige!' said Ashley. 'You look awful! Have you been dancing in your sleep?'

'Feels like it,' I said, trying to catch Ellie's eye.

'Have some snakes,' Ashley said. 'Riley's hiding them, I think.'

'Am not,' said Riley. 'I saw them over by your bag.'

'I'm going to go warm up,' announced Ellie. She left the dressing room, but she did give me a long look as she passed by.

I felt a tiny twitch of hope. She seemed worried.

Riley watched Ellie go. 'Are you guys okay?' she asked.

'No,' I said, sitting down because I felt shaky. 'Not really.'

'Paige!' said Ashley. 'What's wrong? You don't look good at all!'

'I'm just really tired,' I said, glancing at the pack of lollies. 'I don't think even jelly snakes will fix me.'

'Whoa,' Ashley said. 'That *is* serious. Snakes fix everything!'

'Is it Ellie?' asked Riley.

'No,' I said. 'I . . . I don't know.'

My head was all muddled. I hadn't slept properly for the past few nights. I was stressed out because I was really behind on my homework and I hated not knowing what was going on in class (it was hard enough trying to stay awake!). My brain felt tired and my body felt even worse.

Everything was becoming too much and I had nothing to look forward to, just dance, dance, dance, dance.

Ashley sat next to me and put her arm around my shoulders. 'Hey, this isn't right. You're supposed to be the one who looks after everyone else!' she joked.

I giggled a little. 'I know.'

Ashley stood and poked her bum at me. 'Does my wedgie cheer you up?' she asked.

'That makes her throw up,' said Riley. 'Seriously, Paige, do you want me to go get someone?'

'No, thanks,' I said. 'You go to class. I'll be out in a minute.'

'Sure?' asked Riley.

'Yes,' I said.

'Okay,' she said. 'I'll save you a spot next to me.'

'That's if my wedgie doesn't eat it up first,' Ashley said.

Riley threw a snake at her. 'Stop talking about your wedgie!'

'It's taking over my life!' Ashley laughed.

Kind of like dance was taking over mine. I almost preferred Ashley's wedgie.

Once they'd gone I sat in the dressing room by myself. I took some deep breaths. I told myself I just had to get through three things: the ballroom comp, the end of term, and the stupid ballet masterclass. Then I would be okay.

But I don't know if I believed it.

I pulled my slippers on and headed out into the hallway. I still felt dizzy and muddled. I couldn't remember if I'd eaten anything today.

I stood at the studio door and stared at the girls.

But all I saw was a week of dance. Ballroom on Friday, stepping on Benji's toes. Lyrical on Saturday morning, left with no partner because Ellie chose Serah over me. Extra rehearsals on Sunday for my masterclass audition. Ballet on Monday, Ms McGlone scolding me because my shoulders kept creeping up. Extra ballroom rehearsal on Tuesday, still messing up the lift. Jazz on Wednesday, where I forgot the steps and the whole class had to keep repeating the same sequence just for me. Tap straight after that, clack, clack, clack. And now, technique class.

And I couldn't do it. I couldn't face Ellie not looking at me even once. I couldn't bear the thought of being the only person who couldn't do a front aerial with straight legs. My legs felt like jelly just thinking about the floor work.

So I ran away.

Chapter Ten

I didn't really know where I was going. I just kept on running – through the dark halls of Silver Shoes, across the thick carpet, and in and out of the colours cast by the stained-glass windows, until I ended up next to the store-room for props.

The door was unlocked. I opened it and crept in.

It smelled like old paint, mothballs and the sweetness of dried lavender. That was from the 'Welcome Spring' lyrical dance last year, where we all had cane baskets of dried flowers.

It was dark inside. I stumbled around until I collapsed onto a pile of old velvet, which was from the 'Sleeping Beauty' concert years ago. I'd played Aurora. It was probably my only starring role.

I sprawled onto my back and looked at the weird shapes looming around me.

It was quiet and still. I felt far, far away from Silver Shoes and a best friend who didn't look at me. I let my mind be empty of masterclasses and competitions, and boys who I felt embarrassed and clumsy around, even though they were really cool and nice.

I tried not to think about letting down my mum, who just wanted me to be a ballroom star like her.

I tried not to think that I didn't like dancing anymore.

Dancing was something Ellie and I had both loved since we were in kindergarten. Silver Shoes was my favourite place in the whole world, and being on stage was the best feeling, even though my nerves sometimes made me wish I was elsewhere!

I loved dancing, I really did. But here I was, curled up on some mouldy velvet in a dark storeroom, in the back corner of my dance school, avoiding a class that I probably needed more than anyone else!

I don't know how long I was lying there, looking at old papier-mâché drawbridges, piles of cane baskets and cardboard cut-outs of trees. I was so focused on trying to push some energy back into my body that it took me a while to notice whispering outside the door.

'She has to be in there, there's nowhere else.'

'But have you been inside? It's gross.'

'I hope she's okay.'

'Should we go in?'

'You go first.'

Silence.

'No, you better.'

'Okay.'

'Well, hurry up!'

The door opened a crack. Another silence.

'Paige?'

'She's not in here. Come on, let's try the swings.'

'She's here.'

'How do you know?'

'I just know.'

'Paige?'

Three heads poked around the door. Ashley. Riley. And Ellie.

'I'm here.' I sat up with a sigh.

'Oh, we found you!' Ashley came barrelling into me and gave me a big hug. 'Why are you in this stinky place?'

'Why aren't you in class?' I asked. 'You'll get in trouble.'

'Miss Caroline and Jay let us out to come find you,' said Ashley.

'Miss Caroline's worried about you,' added Riley. 'We are, too.'

'I didn't want to make a fuss,' I said. 'I-I . . . couldn't go to class. I needed a break.'

'Well, just be like Riley and miss the start of every class because you have basketball or athletics or something,' said Ashley.

Riley threw a bunch of dried lavender at her.

I noticed Ellie hadn't moved from the doorway.

'Paige,' said Riley, 'I know I'm the worst person to tell you this, but you need to cut back on classes. Something obviously isn't right!'

'And you're hiding in here when you could be doing fun stuff like ten straddle jumps in a row,' Ashley said, grimacing. She paused. 'Actually, you might be onto something. I bags the storeroom next class.'

'I know I need to cut back on stuff,' I said, 'but I don't want to let anyone down.'

'You mean your mum?' Riley asked.

I looked down at my hands.

'You're not even that interested in ballet,' Riley said. 'Why are you doing the masterclass audition on Sunday? Just say you don't want to do it, and that you'd rather focus on jazz or ballroom or something.'

'I'm trying to,' I said, 'but it's hard. I know Mum will be upset.'

There was a big sigh from the doorway.

And then, finally, Ellie talked to me.

'Paige, you big dumbo. What's more important? Your mum being a bit upset when you tell her, or you being like a zombie all the time and running away from class?'

She looked around and wrinkled her nose. 'Plus, you've gotta stop hanging out in storerooms. It's so dark and gross.'

She gave me a smile that made her green eyes crinkle.

I didn't even notice the darkness. My heart did ten jetés. I think, finally, my best friend had come back.

Chapter Eleven

A big white building with too many windows.

Girls stretching everywhere, their hair in impossibly tight buns.

Scary-looking adults walking around with faces that don't know how to smile.

I was at the one place I *never* wanted to be.

An audition.

And, to make it worse, an audition at Dance Art Academy.

The only thing my body wanted to do was sleep, not perform an audition piece that I'd only put together in the last week.

And not very well, at that.

Before that even happened, everyone still had to do a warm-up class where all the teachers from the Royal Academy of Ballet judged you on how well you took direction, and your natural ability.

Maybe I could shove myself into a corner where no one would look at me.

Mum and I went to register at reception, but I was too busy checking out Dance Art to take much notice.

'Paige Montreal,' Mum said to the woman behind the desk. 'Here for the masterclass.'

I could feel Mum's hand on my back while the lady tried to find my name on her list. It took forever. I started to hope that maybe Mum had forgotten to enrol me after all.

But no such luck.

'Oh, here you are,' said the lady. 'Yes. Paige. After the warm-up class you will be in the second audition block. That's at eleven o'clock. Fiona will call you to the waiting area when you're up.' She pointed at another lady who looked like she was born to hate ballerinas.

Great.

It would have been so good to have Ashley by my side, making silly jokes about everyone. Or Ellie, whose confidence always made me feel better.

Mum handed me a sticker that I had to put on my leotard. Number 23.

'This is so exciting, Paigey,' she said, guiding me down the hall. 'I bet you can't wait. Do you want to find a spare room to practise your audition piece before the warm-up?'

'No,' I said. 'I'm okay.'

Dance Art was so scary-looking! Such high ceilings. Floors made of marble that looked like they were cleaned every hour. (Meanwhile, Silver Shoes had dust bunnies behind every door.) There were also huge framed pictures hanging on the walls of every single competition Dance Art had ever won. They were the only splashes of colour in the place. Everything else was so white and bright. It hurt my eyes.

And my tummy.

Mum led me down about a million corridors before we finally reached the audition space. Get this – it was a ballroom! One that looked like it held fancy-dress balls a hundred years ago. What did Dance Art use *that* for?

There was a huge group of girls and a few boys gathered around the double doors. Some were even lined up down the stairs, doing their stretches against the balustrade.

Why were they so keen to get to the audition? All I wanted to do was run away!

'Are you sure you don't need to warm-up, Paigey?' asked Mum. 'I think you should.'

'It's too crowded,' I said.

Although the truth was that if I even moved my body in the smallest way, I felt like my breakfast would come up.

I hunted around for Riley and spotted her, away from the door, which made me feel a tiny bit better.

I had to push past to get to her, and I'd barely said hello before we were called into the ballroom for the first part of the audition.

The ballroom was more than big enough to fit all of us, so of course I had nowhere to hide. They let us line up wherever we wanted, and I quickly took a place next to Riley.

Straightaway I needed to pee.

I was stressing out so much, I didn't even really hear the Royal Academy people introduce themselves.

Was my ribbon tight enough? Was my posture good? Were those girls over there staring at me, waiting for me to mess up?

This is only a warm-up, Paige, I told myself. *You've done these steps a million times before.*

We began with barre work, moving into the five positions, demi pliés and grand pliés, relevés, and then leg stretches – coupé, posse, ronds de jambe and battements. It was so familiar to me that I began to relax.

I could do this, couldn't I?

Chapter Twelve

Turns out I could.

Everyone spilled out of the ballroom and down the stairs. I slipped to one side and took a big breath. I hadn't fallen on my face. No one had pointed and laughed at my sickled feet or bent back knee and I hadn't crashed into anyone on the travelling steps.

But my legs and arms felt loose and wobbly, as if there was nothing inside holding my body together.

I stumbled over to the water cooler and took a paper cup.

Jasmine was already there, taking tiny sips. Her face was quite red and she looked very frazzled and un-Jasminey.

'Hi Jasmine,' I said, not really expecting her to talk back.

'Hey,' she said.

'How did you go?' I asked.

It was funny – because we were both from Silver Shoes, I felt like we were kind of in it together. Like we had to represent our dance school.

'I think I went okay,' Jasmine said. She crumpled the empty cup in her hand. 'I hope so, anyway.'

'You're a really good ballerina,' I said. 'I reckon you have a great chance of getting in.'

Jasmine clasped her hands together and gave me a small, shaky smile. 'Thanks, Paige.

I really want a place in the masterclass, so that means a lot.'

Riley came by then and grabbed my arm. 'Paige!' she said. 'I need some sugar. Let's go find some snakes.'

I waved goodbye to Jasmine, wished her good luck and let Riley pull me along. It felt nice to be around my friend. Riley was so unfazed by the whole thing. I know it was mean, but I also felt a bit better seeing how even perfect dancers like Jasmine could get nervous, too. It didn't excuse her snippy comments, but it was nice to see what was beneath all that.

We found Mum pacing around down the hall and dug the snakes out of her hand-bag. She asked a million questions about the warm-up, and Riley answered them all while devouring the lollies. I managed half a snake and then my tummy felt sick again.

It was because of the girls around me. They were so pretty and they didn't look scared one bit. I watched some of them warm up. It was like they were made of rubber; they were so flexible. You could easily mistake them as members of the Royal Academy of Ballet already.

What was I doing here?

'Paige?'

I blinked. 'Pardon?'

Riley giggled. 'I said, do you want to find a studio and we can go over our audition pieces?'

'Oh,' I said. 'Sure.'

'Should I come along?' asked Mum. 'I can give you some last-minute pointers.'

'I think we'll be right,' I said. 'Go and have a coffee, Mum.'

'Yeah, looks like they have a whole restaurant down there,' said Riley.

'Well, if you're sure,' said Mum. She kissed Riley on the cheek and then gave me a big perfumey cuddle. 'Best of luck to you, girls. You'll both be gorgeous and knock them dead. I know it.'

'Thanks, Mrs Montreal,' said Riley before taking my arm and leading me into a nearby studio.

'How ya doin', Paige?' she asked.

I just looked at her.

'Oh yep.' Riley laughed. 'Got it.'

She started to practise her audition piece, which was full of her perfect grande jetés, brisés and arabesques, which her long legs made look effortless. I was so nervous that I couldn't even get my legs to swap once in my entrechats.

In the end my tummy got so flip-floppy and my legs so shaky, that I went back to the waiting area outside the lobby and sat down.

The mean-looking lady from reception raised an eyebrow at me.

'You're not in for a while,' she said.

'I know,' I squeaked.

Riley joined me and sat back against the wall, rolling out her ankles. How could she be so calm? I swear I had beans. Every new position I sat in was more uncomfortable than the last. I fiddled and twitched all the way through the first lot of girls doing their audition.

And then it was our turn.

A girl I recognised from Dance Art was first.

Then Riley was called in.

And the third person was . . .

Me.

Chapter Thirteen

'Paige Montreal?'

I looked up.

'Paige?' said the mean lady, looking over her glasses at me.

'Yes?' I squeaked.

'You're up next,' said Mean Eyes.

'Okay.'

The remaining girls in our block looked at me like I was a weirdo. I got to my feet.

I walked towards the scary, massive ballroom doors.

They opened and Riley came out. She was beaming and had two big red spots on her cheeks.

'Paige!' she said breathlessly. 'Are you next?'

'Yes,' I whispered. One-word answers were all I could manage.

'It's fun!' said Riley.

Yeah, right.

'I'd wait for you, but I have to hurry up, Nana's waiting to take me to Ash's hip hop gig.'

I nodded.

'Paige,' huffed Mean Eyes. 'You may go in now.'

'You'll be fine,' said Riley. 'They're not too scary at all. Just dance like you always do.'

'Thanks.'

'See ya soon?' she asked.

I nodded again before I watched her disappear.

'They're *waiting* for you,' said Mean Eyes. Her voice could have snuffed out a candle.

I went in.

I tried to make my feet as soft as possible, but I swear a herd of elephants came tramping in with me.

Gosh. As if the ballroom wasn't large enough when we were all in there. Now it was just me, I felt like I was in a castle.

Right at the end was a long table. Three people were sitting behind it: the man and woman who'd led the warm-up, and another lady who looked very old. She wore a huge floral scarf that swallowed her whole head.

My feet slowed. I came to a halt.

Silence.

'You can come closer, dear,' said Floral Scarf.

I moved forward one step.

Mr and Mrs Warm-Up looked at each other. Then Mr Warm-Up leaned on his elbow.

'Well, hello,' he said.

'Hello,' I went to say, but my spit got all slippery in my mouth. I swallowed and cleared my throat. 'Hello,' I tried again. My voice was meant to sound bright and cheery.

It was a miserable failure.

'So you're Paige,' said Mr Warm-Up.

Obviously, said Ellie's voice in my head.

I snorted back a giggle and tried to stand straighter.

'We saw you in warm-up,' he continued. 'There was a lovely lightness to your movements, although you need to keep your shoulders down. There's a lot of tension around the back of your neck. I understand you're probably a bit nervous.'

'There's no need to be anxious, dear,' said Floral Scarf.

I clasped my hands together. My palms were clammy. Floral Scarf and Mr and Mrs Warm-Up kept coming in and out of focus.

'It says on your audition form you do a lot of styles,' said Mrs Warm-Up. 'You must be a busy girl. What's your favourite?'

Mind blank. All my words were stuck somewhere between my tummy and my throat.

I remembered I was supposed to be making a good impression.

'Ballet,' I said.

'Of course,' said Mr Warm-Up with a mean smile.

'And why would you like a place in this masterclass?' asked Mrs Warm-Up.

Well, here's the thing. I don't. I don't want to be here at all. Ballet isn't my favourite style. And I hate auditions. Also, your sweater is really ugly.

I just couldn't lie. Not anymore. I couldn't even think of the first step in my audition piece. And even if I could, I knew I wasn't going to perform it well.

Because my heart wasn't in it. And that's where dancing should come from.

'Actually, it's fine if I don't get a place,' I answered.

'Beg your pardon?' asked Mrs Warm-Up. She leaned back in her chair and gaped at Mr Warm-Up and Floral Scarf. But Floral Scarf didn't even look at her. Instead she leaned forward and rested her chin on her hand.

'Go on, dear,' she said.

'It doesn't matter if I don't get a place,' I said, a little more clearly. 'It's best it goes to somebody who actually wants to do the masterclass. Excuse me.'

What was I doing? I was turning to leave the audition! Was I really?

'Thank you for your time,' I added quickly, dropping a curtsy. And then I left.

'Heh heh heh,' I heard Floral Scarf say as I ran out. 'I like that one. Should have done that years ago myself.'

Chapter Fourteen

When I got home that night Mum was sitting up at the kitchen bench, tapping her gold fingernails against the surface.

Clack, clack, clack.

'Hi,' I said, shutting the front door.

'Did you have a good time at the concert?' Her nose wrinkled. 'The hip hop one.'

'Yes, thank you,' I said, hanging up my dance bag. 'Ash and Benji were really good.'

'I wish you'd checked with me before you rushed off with Riley,' Mum said.

Clack, clack, clack.

'I'm sorry,' I said, 'but I had to race down after my audition. They were pulling out of the car park when I saw them. I didn't have time to find you, so I thought it would be okay to send you a text on Mrs Nason's phone.'

'Yes, well, I appreciate that,' said Mum, 'but we didn't agree you could go. The audition was the most important thing. You're lucky it finished in time.'

I looked down at my feet. 'Very lucky.'

Clack, clack, clack.

'Where's Dad?' I asked, watching her fingernails.

'He's in the garden.'

Clack.

'I think I'm going to take a shower,' I said.

'Paige,' said Mum.

'Yes?'

'Anything else you want to tell me?'

Clack.

'I don't think so,' I whispered.

'Anything about the audition?'

'Umm . . .'

'Like how you ran out of it?'

Silence. Mum looked at me like I'd just said dancing was the worst thing in the whole world.

I sighed.

'Did you really think I wouldn't find out? Paige, you worked so hard on that audition piece!' She stood up, her hands on her hips.

'Not as hard I could have,' I said, 'if I wasn't already dancing so much.'

'Pardon?'

'I only finished learning my piece a few days ago,' I explained. 'I wasn't ready. Just like I'm not ready for the ballroom comp next weekend.'

'It's a shame,' said Mum, as if she hadn't heard me at all, 'but there is another masterclass coming up in a few months with the Australian Dance Company. We can work towards that one.' She sat back down with her hands tightly clasped on the bench.

'I don't want to do that either,' I said.

Mum got up again and switched the kettle on. 'What did you say, sweetie?' she asked, looking for the tea bags.

'Mum! I don't want to do any more ballet masterclasses!'

She looked in the cupboard for some cups. 'Do you want a hot chocolate?' she asked.

'Mum!' I said, louder this time.

My cheeks were burning up and I felt a bit sick, but I knew I had to say it again. 'I'm not going to do any more ballet masterclasses! And I'm not going to do the ballroom competition either!'

Mum turned around and gave me a long look. The two cups in her hands said 'Born to Dance' on them.

'I'm not quite sure what you mean,' she said. 'I'm very disappointed you ran out of that audition, you know. It doesn't look good. That masterclass could have been a great opportunity for you.'

'Yes, but I haven't even decided I want to be a ballerina,' I said. 'I don't know if it's my favourite style. I'm not even that good at it.'

'Of course you are,' said Mum, 'and it's a great foundation for your ballroom work.'

'But I'm doing so many classes and all these competitions and masterclasses and it's too much! I don't have time to try to be really good at one or discover which one I like the best. It's just dance, dance, dance!'

'I thought you wanted to be an all-rounder,' said Mum.

'I do,' I said, 'but I also want to discover my special style. Like, Ellie has Broadway, Riley has ballet, Ash has hip hop, and they all have so much fun. I want to just enjoy what I'm dancing and then hopefully I'll love it so much that I'll *want* to do the competitions and everything.' I took a deep breath. 'Not be forced to.'

'I don't force you!' cried Mum. She looked down at the cups in her hands. 'Do I?'

'I don't want to let you down,' I mumbled, 'because I know you love dancing, too, and it's probably nice to see me in things, but . . .' I looked up at her and grinned. 'Maybe you should take some dance lessons again! Miss Caroline is starting an adults' group. She was talking about it the other day.'

Mum looked at me for a long time and then she laughed. 'Maybe I should,' she said. 'I'm sorry if you thought I was pressuring you, Paigey. I just love watching you dance. You're beautiful on stage. It makes me so proud, honey.'

'I know,' I said.

Mum stared at the 'Born to Dance' cups. 'So you don't want to do the ballroom comp on Sunday?'

'We're not ready for it,' I said. 'Have you seen our standing spins?'

Mum smothered a smile. 'Hmm, you might have a point.'

'Plus, I really want to go to Ellie's birthday,' I said.

'Yes, you should do that,' Mum said. 'Your friends are important. But do you still want to continue with the ballroom lessons?' she asked hopefully.

'Yeah,' I said, 'I'm enjoying them. I just need more practice, though. So I can get really good.'

Mum smiled. 'And Benji's rather cute, isn't he?'

'Mum!' I said. My skin got all itchy and hot.

'Whoo, is that a blush, honey?' she teased.

Dad came strolling through the front door then, covered in mud and bits of weed. There was a leaf in his hair. He looked at Mum and then at the cups.

'Brilliant,' he said. 'A cuppa's just what I need.'

Chapter Fifteen

On Sunday night I had the biggest, best sleep I'd had in a long time.

I saw Riley in ballet class on Monday and told her what I'd decided. She gave me a big hug. 'Awesome, Paige,' she said. 'It was very brave of you.'

'Well, it was either that or I become the first dancing zombie,' I joked.

Jasmine walked by us with Tove, as usual,

a step behind her. I saw straightaway that the nice, nervous Jasmine from the auditions was gone. Back at Silver Shoes, she was the Queen again.

'Heard you ran out of the audition yesterday, Paige,' she said with a sickly sweet smile. 'I hope nothing bad happened.'

'Yeah, not till now, when we saw you,' said Riley.

'So funny,' Jasmine said.

'Haha,' added Tove.

'No, nothing bad happened,' I said. 'In fact, it was exactly the opposite. But I hope you do well, Jasmine. I'm sure you did a great audition.'

Jasmine looked taken aback, but I always find it easier just to be nice to her. Plus I'm not like Ellie, Riley and Ash – I can't think of snappy things to say.

'Anyway,' said Riley, 'Paige doesn't need to worry about the masterclass. She'll have enough work to do with the mid-year showcase. She got the last spot.'

'What?' said Jasmine.

'But we were going to do a duo!' said Tove.

'Oh well,' said Riley, 'I guess people have had enough of the circus.'

Jasmine and Tove are famous for their over-the-top duos. By themselves they're great dancers, but put them together and something strange happens. Everything becomes big – big themes, big characters, big dancing. Ellie and I have danced against them in duos a few times, and we haven't lost yet.

'What will you be performing?' asked Jasmine, crossing her arms.

'It's a surprise,' I said.

'You don't know what you're doing yet?' said Tove.

'No, stupid, she means she's going to surprise us,' Jasmine huffed.

'Oh,' said Tove.

'What's the point of that?' said Jasmine. 'No one will watch anyway.'

'You don't need to worry about it,' said Riley, 'seeing as you're obviously a shoo-in for the masterclass.' She grabbed my arm and dragged me away.

Benji's hip hop performance yesterday had got me thinking. Watching him dance was brilliant! When you're dancing opposite someone, like I do with Benji in ballroom practice, you sometimes don't notice how good they are. But when you watch them perform . . . wow. That's a different story.

Benji really deserved to have people see how talented he was. So I'd made him a deal. Neither of us wanted to do our waltz in the ballroom competition, so we'd made our stand – no to the comp. But there was one spot left in the mid-year showcase. It was four weeks away . . . surely that would give us enough time to perfect our waltz?

'It isn't your mum telling you, or your dance teacher, or anyone else forcing you to do it,' I'd said to him. 'It's just me, asking you. We'll have lots of practice by then. And I really want all my friends at Silver Shoes to see what a great dance partner I have.'

That last bit made me embarrassed and I couldn't look at him when I'd said it.

But he'd agreed!

'Keep it a secret,' I said. 'I want it to be a surprise. For my mum and my friends and everyone. I'll just tell everyone else I'm doing a solo. Only Miss Caroline will know.'

So that was one secret I was keeping.

But I had another.

One I hoped would make my best friend very, very happy.

Chapter Sixteen

The butterflies in my tummy were almost as big as when I had a performance.

'You have a great time, sweetie,' Mum called to me out the car window. She nodded at the present I had in my hands. 'Ellie will love it.'

She blew me a kiss and drove off. It was just me and my second secret.

That I was coming to Ellie's eleventh birthday party, after all.

Right now Ellie thought I was at the ballroom competition. But there was no way I was going to miss my best friend's birthday.

So I'd decided to surprise her. I'd made Riley and Ash keep the secret, too. Ellie and I had been talking all this week at Silver Shoes, and things were almost back to normal at school. But I knew she was disappointed that I couldn't make it to her party.

It was hard to keep a secret from my best friend, especially when I knew if I told her, she'd be back to her laughing, loving, hugging self.

But the surprise would make it all worth it.

'Don't forget you have to wear pink,' Ash had reminded me. 'The invitation was very clear about that. And it's a dance party. So who knows what that means, but don't wear uncomfortable shoes.'

I was wearing a long, pale pink fuzzy sweater with a ballerina in the corner, over black tights and my pink and silver ballet flats. Ellie had given me the sweater last Christmas. The funny thing was that I'd given her the same one, only in hot pink.

I tucked Ellie's present under my arm and headed round the side of the house, along the path where we'd played chasings a million times and been in trouble for squashing Mrs Irvin's lilies.

The music coming from the backyard was a mix of Ellie's favourite pop songs and musical theatre tunes. When I rounded the corner my face broke out in the hugest smile. The backyard had been Ellie-fied.

Pink balloons and glittery streamers had been added wherever they would fit – they were flying off Ellie's little brother's swing set, the fence, the benches and the garden gnomes.

Mrs Irvin's gazebo was covered in pink fairy lights and there were posters of Ellie's favourite dancers covering the walls. Next to the gazebo a makeshift dance floor had been set up, and in the corner of the garden Ellie's old dance costumes were hanging off the washing line.

I stood looking at it all, so happy to be there. I spotted Ellie over by the dance floor, surrounded by girls from school. She was in her favourite place – the centre of attention. And she was wearing her pink sweater, too.

Someone knocked into me, growling like a dinosaur. I looked down.

'Paige!' screamed Lucas, Ellie's little brother. He wrapped his arms around my waist.

'Paige!' yelled out Riley and Ash, jumping up from the swing set. Ash almost got knocked out by a balloon. 'You're here!'

'Paige?' said Ellie. She stared at me from where she was standing.

'Hi,' I gave a small wave. Suddenly I felt very shy.

'Grrrrrrrr,' growled Lucas. He looked back at me and Ellie. 'You're matching!'

'Paige!' Ellie said again.

And then she came rushing towards me and gave me the biggest hug. It had to be at least three weeks' worth.

'Oww!' cried Lucas, squished between us.

'You made it!' Ellie said.

'Of course I did.'

'But the ballroom competition?'

I shrugged. 'I'd rather be here.'

Ellie hugged me again. 'I'm so glad that you are,' she said. 'It wouldn't have been the same without you.'

'Everything looks great,' I said.

Ellie pointed at my sweater, laughing. '*You* look great.'

I giggled. 'So do you.'

'What about me?' asked Lucas.

'You look gorgeous!' said Ash, running in and scooping him up. He squealed and reached out his arms for Riley. 'Welcome to the party, Paige.'

'Happy Birthday, Ellie,' I said.

Phew. One secret down.

One to go.

Chapter Seventeen

Mid-year showcase time!

Silver Shoes was turned into the performance space of the century, right before our eyes.

There are three main studios at Silver Shoes – two big ones, which are where the main parts of the church used to be, and then a smaller one out the back (where Benji and I had been practising our ballroom).

But then there's the hall at the side of Silver

Shoes, which has a big old raised stage. Lovely swooshy curtains hang down either side of it and a set of stairs at each end lead down into the hall part where the audience sits.

Mum was on the Silver Shoes committee, so of course I was there with her at ten o'clock in the morning, preparing Silver Shoes for the performance that night.

First I had to help her line up the costume racks in the ballroom studio, which was going to be our dressing room (our usual one was just too small). Then I had to check that every single costume was there, and go hunting in the crowded costume closet for missing bows and felt hats.

Next she tried to get me to help make the sandwiches for lunch, but I quickly passed that off to Ellie, who laughed and said I'd better watch out because she'd put snails in mine.

Then, along with Riley (who got into the masterclass, by the way!), I had to help put out all the seats in the hall, after we'd swept the floors with this massive broom. But we were quickly sent away because we started trying to sweep each other up instead.

Finally I had to go and help Ash decorate the reception area. And all this while I was on and off of the stage, rehearsing the dances and going through the running order.

Well, every dance but my secret one. I'd tucked my costume away in the corner of the costume room. I couldn't wait to dance in it for the first time.

There was this amazing feeling of excitement in all the halls and studios, of the teachers, parents and students preparing for the mid-year showcase at Silver Shoes. Everyone couldn't wait to perform what they'd been working on all year. I felt happy, and I *wanted* to perform and dance tonight. It was such a great feeling to have back.

All too soon we were being hurried into the third studio to get ready for the performance. The older girls at Silver Shoes were looking after the tinies, playing games with them and doing their make-up. They were soooo cute! One group was dressed in dinosaur onesies for their dance, the 'Dinosaur Stomp'.

'Oh gosh,' said Ellie. 'After seeing this, Lucas is gonna want to join Silver Shoes, I just know it.'

'He'd be a great dancer,' I said, applying my eyeliner. Out of the corner of my eye I saw someone poke their head around the studio door. 'Oh!' I said. 'Back in a sec. Just have to . . . check my costume.'

I ran out and down the hall.

'Benji?' I whispered.

He stepped out from behind an old wall heater. 'What's up?' he asked. 'I came round the back, like you said.'

'Thank you so much for doing this!' I was so excited, I gave him a hug.

'Oh,' he stammered. 'Yeah . . . that's cool. Yeah. It'll be fun.'

'Really?' I asked.

'Yep.' He nodded. 'No, really. I'm glad you asked me. It'll be good practice for when we win that next ballroom comp, right?'

'Well, we have improved!' I said. 'I'm so glad my friends will get to see you dance. Everyone's gonna want you to join Silver Shoes, now.'

Benji shoved his hands in his pockets. 'Yeah, I'm thinking about it,' he said with a smile.

I clapped my hands. 'The program says we're on near the end of the first act. So just hang around if you like. If anyone asks, say you're helping out.'

'Cool,' said Benji. He grinned. 'Thanks, Paige.'

The next hour passed so quickly. It was a blur of dancing on stage and changing costumes. First I was in Birdy's 'Skinny Love' for my lyrical class. We wore these elaborate medieval-style velvet dresses and Miss Caroline's idea for the dance was to 'imagine we were butterflies, or a dying shooting star, and this was our last grasp at life'.

Things cheered up when we did Pharrell Williams' 'Happy' for jazz. Our costume was a bright glittery shift dress, and the dance was set in the 1960s motown era, with lots of claps, swinging and grooving. What a difference to be in the moment, enjoying myself, and knowing exactly what I had to do, instead of worrying about my waltz!

Before I knew it, it was almost waltz time. I rushed into the costume room to get ready for my surprise ballroom performance with Benji.

Gosh. I'd forgotten how beautiful the dress was. As soon as I pulled it on and was surrounded by all the layers of yellow and gold, and the little butterflies and beads, I felt like I was a part of something special and that the dress would become an extension of my movements.

'Wow,' said a voice. 'You look amazing.'

I turned to see my tin soldier, Benji, waiting for me by the door.

'Thank you,' I said. 'You look very handsome.'

This time he blushed!

He gave a silly little bow and I took his arm and got ready to complete surprise number two.

Chapter Eighteen

Dancing my waltz with Benji on the Silver Shoes stage, I realised it was probably the first time I actually really loved ballroom.

And do you know why?

It wasn't just because all my friends and the people I loved were watching me.

Or because there was no pressure to win anything.

Or because, for once, I actually felt like I knew the routine I was performing.

It was because I wanted to be there. I was excited to show off my dancing, and what I'd worked so hard learning.

And because I was having fun.

I remembered why dancing was such a magical thing.

As soon as our waltz music, 'Greensleeves', began playing, a silence fell over the audience. I started my fouetté turns, and every time I went around I caught a sparkle from the butterflies in my hair.

After I couldn't fouetté anymore, and I had collapsed on the ground (acting, of course!), out came Benji as the tin soldier.

He picked me up and we went into our closed hold. Just before he began to lead into our driving step, he did the biggest, cheekiest grin, like he was about to have the best time.

My heart melted, or maybe it was the fairy ballerina's. And we began to waltz.

It really seemed like Benji and I were going round and round in a music box. Sometime during our dance I noticed Ellie, Riley and Ash had come to the side of the stage. They were huddled in the wings, watching us.

Forget about box steps and underarm right turns, whisks and promenade to close. It was just the story of the fairy ballerina and her tin soldier. There was also this new, nice feeling that I hadn't had before.

It was trust. Trusting your partner. I finally knew what Fleur meant when she kept calling out, 'Paige, Benji! Where is your connection? You must have connection!'

Connection didn't mean touching someone. It meant trusting them. And ballroom made that really clear.

Mum had found a version of 'Greensleeves' where the music at the end actually slowed

down in tempo, like it does when the music box runs out.

Benji and I began to turn slower and slower, until eventually I stopped moving and stood still. Benji bowed to me, as if to thank me for the dance, and then the lights faded as he walked offstage.

I blinked. I took a big breath. I stood in the darkness, slowly becoming Paige again, and not the fairy ballerina.

Then Benji was fumbling for my hand and the lights came back on. We walked to the front of the stage for our bows.

Fleur and Miss Caroline were clapping and cheering louder than anyone. Miss Caroline tipped me a wink that said, 'You pulled it off, Paige!'

Mum was sitting next to them. When I caught her eye, she put one hand on her chest and blew me a kiss.

Her eyes were teary and I realised she was doing an embarrassing Mum cry. Usually it's Riley's mum who does that. It's kind of a joke between us four girls – whose mum will cry this time?

Speaking of us four girls, suddenly Benji and I were surrounded by the excited cheers of Ellie, Riley and Ash. Even before we'd got offstage they were jumping all over us and squeezing us to bits.

Poor Benji.

But that's how it was at Silver Shoes.

And I never wanted to be anywhere else.

Paige Montreal

Full name: Paige Elizabeth Montreal

Nickname: Paigey

Age: 10

Favourite dance styles: Lyrical and ballroom

Best friend: Ellie

Family: Mum and Dad

Favourite colours: Yellow and emerald green

Favourite food: Jelly snakes, raisin toast

Favourite school subject: Art

Hobbies: Dancing, writing stories, drawing, art and craft (I help Mum make her jewellery!), collecting Cabbage Patch dolls

What I want to be when I grow up: Dancer or teacher

Best dancing moment: When Ellie and I did a 'Beach Babes' duo as tinies and became best friends

Things I love: Dancing, going on holidays to tropical Queensland, playing with our puppy Brie, staying over at Ellie's house, cooking dinner with Dad when Mum has a 'girls' night', sleeping in (and Ellie wants me to say 'Benji', but I won't!)

How to do a Perfect Closed Hold

The closed hold is the most common hold in ballroom dancing. Partners stand facing each other, with the man's right hand on the lady's back, near her left shoulder blade. The couple's other hands are clasped together around chest- or shoulder-height.

Tip

Stand tall, with your head up and shoulders relaxed.

How to do a Perfect Promenade Hold

The promenade hold is a V-shaped position with the man's left side and the lady's right side slightly open, allowing the couple to walk forward. The man's head should be turned to the left; the lady's to the right. Hand positions are the same as for a closed hold.

Tip

To begin, make sure your feet are in third position rather than first or second.